RETURN TO THE SUN

TOM ANDERSON

Return to the Sun
Published in Great Britain in 2022
by Graffeg Limited.

Written by Tom Anderson copyright © 2022.
Designed and produced by Graffeg Limited copyright
© 2022.

Graffeg Limited, 24 Stradey Park Business Centre,
Mwrwg Road, Llangennech, Llanelli,
Carmarthenshire, SA14 8YP, Wales, UK.
Tel: 01554 824000. www.graffeg.com.

Tom Anderson is hereby identified as the author
of this work in accordance with section 77 of the
Copyrights, Designs and Patents Act 1988.

A CIP Catalogue record for this book is available from
the British Library.

This is a work of fiction. Names, characters, places,
and incidents either are the products of the author's
imagination or are used fictitiously.

The publisher acknowledges the financial support of
the Books Council of Wales. www.gwales.com.

Printed and bound in Great Britain by Clays Ltd,
Elcograf S.p.A.

ISBN 9781802580853

1 2 3 4 5 6 7 8 9

RETURN TO THE SUN

TOM ANDERSON

GRAFFEG

Prologue

There was just over two minutes left, and Chloe needed a 5.8 to take the win. Absolutely within her abilities. She could hear the beach announcer saying something, but it was in a lower voice, so that the spectators could hear it but not the competitors in the line-up. Chloe had priority – the next wave was hers, whatever anyone else did, and she was stalking the take-off zone with confidence. If the right one came, she knew she would be European Champion.

She started doing the maths in her head. She always did when there was only two minutes left. *How often were the sets coming through? What was the interval?*

It wasn't nerves. Not yet. Ninety seconds left and still a decent chance for the ocean to send something her way.

But at some point, Chloe knew she'd need to change her plan. How long should she leave it before she decided a bigger one *wasn't* coming?

It was inside the final minute when she started

moving towards shore – 5.8 could be found on a half-way-out wave anyway, at least for her, in the form she was in. At forty seconds she saw the first of the waves she could take. The interval that day was ten seconds, so if she didn't take the first, there would be two more to choose from. She tried to stand on her board in the flats for a moment, raising her head to see what was beyond it. Not enough promise to pass this first wave up. Of course, the perfect choice should be wave three, if she knew it would offer up the length. If she caught that, it would mean her opponents wouldn't have time to catch anything in reply.

But Chloe couldn't be sure either of the next two waves would peel properly, so now she was going to have to take the risk.

First wave of the set it is.

You're overthinking this, she reminded herself. *Take the one you want. Put the pressure back on them anyway, whatever happens. Let them earn it.*

Decision made. She was going. This was her moment. She dug in, paddled hard, popped up and drove down the face. The wave was running off at just the right pace, so she sunk deep into a drawn-out bottom turn, then smacked off the top, twice, with a fan of spray flickering into the air each time. With a big closeout turn her score would be there or thereabouts. She eyed the end section, took aim and glanced off it. Her knees pulled in, and the landing was smooth and fast. She punched the air in front of her with a tight fist – a private gesture, but also just visible enough to tell the judges, *I've done it! Come on! Give me the score!*

She'd done her maths right. There had been time left for three waves to break. And she'd picked a good one.

But what was coming behind her wave, she would have to believe, had been beyond her control.

She would *have* to believe that to ever get over it.

She'd done her job – on the wave she chose.

But she should have gone for wave three. As she kicked out and looked behind her, European Champion for twenty seconds, she felt a lump in her throat. *Please fall off!*

But she knew what had happened. Chloe knew her chance had come and gone in the same three-wave set. If mine was a 5.8, she thought, that girl's there is getting a 6.5. Maybe even more. *Please fall off!*

But she knew that was never going to happen. And she knew what it meant – that she would remember this moment, forever.

For all the wrong reasons.

Chapter 1

'You sure we're actually going somewhere sunnier?' said Chloe, pulling her coat up around her neck as the day lost its last bit of warmth.

'Maybe not today,' said Caio. 'But it won't take long to feel the difference. We went east today, mostly. Tomorrow we can get five whole degrees south.'

'Does that mean it'll be five degrees warmer? Epic. Can't wait.'

Caio looked at his sister as she sunk further into the neck of that coat. 'I haven't got a clue,' he said. 'We're going the right way, though. I know that.'

In most circumstances, standing by a queue of cars and vans that wasn't moving would be a nightmare. Think of traffic jams – the fear of getting stuck, mixed with the boredom. But a ferry queue is nothing of the sort. This is a queue of cars which is expecting, *awaiting*, adventure.

So it was, then, for Chloe and Caio, as the early evening drew in. It was the last week of October. The clocks hadn't quite gone back yet. You could feel the long winter nights were just round the corner, and as the queue faded into the dusk, car light after car light came on. Engines were starting. The boat was ready to load.

*　*　*

It's always hard to decide how to spend time on those crossings, thought Caio. He started predicting what Chloe would want to do. She'd want to go to the bar. Surely that would be her thing. He was more concerned himself about the need to drive again at six in the morning, when they docked. But Chloe? She'd want to try and have some fun, he guessed. She'd want to take the seriousness out of it.

'Can you see the lights there?' she asked him.

'Yeah.'

'Portsmouth. D'you reckon *they* can see *us*?'

'Probably.'

'But are they looking? I mean, did *we* ever look out to sea in all the time we've spent living right next to it?'

Caio looked at boats quite a lot actually, although a ferry this size would be a rare sight going past the sleepy south Wales town where he and Chloe had grown up.

'So I suppose you'll want to go to the bar on Deck Seven, then?' he asked her.

Chloe laughed. 'Nah. Really? We've got a big drive to do. Why would we do that? Let's find somewhere outdoors, look overboard, chuck another handful of Dad's ashes in, and then crash for an early start.'

Wrong again, Caio thought. *I've got her wrong again.*

* * *

As with every other time, the ashes made the situation immediately serious.

'He won't mind where we do it as long as it's a patch of ocean,' Chloe said. 'But I say we still save as much as we can for when we get to the end of the road.'

Caio agreed.

It had been a long day, but getting to sleep still wasn't that easy. Caio rolled and twitched on the bunk below as the boat rose and dropped on the swell.

On the bunk above, Chloe was doing no

better. She tried to line her breath up with the waves. In, out... up, down. She wondered if louder exhales might make Caio think she was out cold. She was older, after all, and needed to show him what calm and responsible should look like.

Eventually, they both gave in to the rolling rhythms of the ocean, and a brief spell of deep slumber kicked in. It was broken sooner than they'd wanted by the ferry-wide alarm.

'Ladies and gentlemen, we will soon be docking in Le Havre. The time is now seven a.m. in France, and may we remind you this is an hour ahead of the UK. Please could you make your way to the vehicle decks for disembarkation.'

Having the last of the bananas they'd brought from home for breakfast, they made their way down to the hold.

'Pass us the key, Chloe,' asked Caio. 'I wanna try and get this bag back in the side door again first.'

'Just use yours.'

'What?'

'I said just use yours.'

'What d'you mean? My key?'

'Yeah, you had a key on your own chain, then. I saw.'

Caio pulled out his keyring. 'It's not for the

van, though.'

'Doesn't matter,' said Chloe.

'What? But this key's for my Audi, back home.'

'So?'

'So it won't work.'

'Yeah, it will.'

Caio spoke louder over the engine noises in case he wasn't being heard: 'It's THE KEY TO MY AUDI. It won't fit. This is a fifteen-year-old VW Kombi!'

'Yeah, I know,' said Chloe. 'But the lock is worn out. It'll open with *any* key.'

'You serious? How safe it that?'

'It's fine,' said Chloe. 'Dad used it like that for years. Quite convenient, really. As long as only our mates know it works that way.'

Caio pushed his Audi key into the side door. Sure enough, it was open. With a groan, he shoved his bag back under the sofa seat and drew the door shut again. It was stuffy down here, he thought, and wound his passenger window open a little.

'It'll be fine,' said Chloe, coming round to his side and tapping Caio's shoulder with a knuckle. 'We'll never get locked out, at least?'

Engines were firing up, and now there was that queue of excited motors once more, but this time inside the stale, metal enclosure of a boat hull. Caio and Chloe did their belts up and then heard the great metallic *clank* of the ferry doors popping open, the winding chains of drawbridges lowering, the rumble of engines finding their gears and vehicles moving forward. Chloe closed the van windows to keep out the exhaust fumes.

Much quicker than it had seemed at the other end, they were moving through lanes and passport control and then remembered to change sides of the road too.

They were in France. They were on the Continent. Now it was time to look ahead at the task they'd been given. They were here to honour the promises they'd made to Dad – to take him, and his van, on a last journey. Yes, time to look ahead at the challenge set.

And the open road.

Chapter 2

'You know, Dad used to say if I tried to marry a bloke who hadn't broken down in a car at the side of the road... then he would stop me. He literally wouldn't let me. He'd refuse his permission. He actually even asked a guy that question once at the front door. *Have you ever broken down in a car, mate? Even running out of petrol can count.*'

'I wouldn't get the nod of approval, then,' said Caio.

'Well, that's not a bad thing, mind,' said Chloe. 'Considering I'm your sister.'

'Half-sister,' Caio reminded her. 'You get judged much less for having a different mum.'

'If you say so. I never noticed it, mind.'

'Whatever.' Caio was leaning a hand out of the window, letting the current outside push it up and down like a body-pop. 'Seriously, though,' he went on. 'What d'you reckon Dad would have said if he knew I hadn't ever broken down? Would he be, like, ashamed?'

Chloe shrugged her shoulders as she flipped on the indicators. 'I wouldn't worry about it. And anyway, you might be about to get that experience this morning. Listen to the state on this thing.'

Caio tuned his ear to the loud vibrations of metal under their feet – it sounded like an engine that hated the cold. Arthritic and stiff, their father's old VW Kombi wasn't a morning kind of vehicle in its old age.

A puff of blue-grey smoke came out of the exhaust.

'Already?' Caio asked. 'It's only late October. How did he drive this thing back home in January?'

'He used to talk to it,' said Chloe. 'He had the knack.'

'Hope you've got that from him, then,' said Caio. 'I certainly haven't. I haven't even driven with a tyre-pressure light on before.'

'Well, that's one thing that's not gonna change, then. Dad cut the wires to all the warning lights years ago. Ah well, we're going south, it'll only get warmer.'

They turned right onto the giant Pont de Normandie bridge, which lifted them into the sky. Caio saw a group of walkers, sticks in hand and backpacks strapped, making their way across on the path beside them. The walkers seemed to be going about the same speed as him and Chloe. Eventually, though, the VW made it to the highest point, and then began the much smoother journey downwards. Under them, the famous River Seine glistened in the late autumn sun. Odd to think this was the same river which slithered in and out of the buildings of Paris a few hundred miles upstream.

Caio pictured what this grand bridge must have looked like from above or below, with him and Chloe trundling along the highest stretch. How far into space would you still see their van's banana yellow awning, with its orange go-faster stripe? And while the light-blue bodywork might have blended into the sky behind, the red lightning bolt which had been sprayed down the side stood out from miles away.

Another mini cloud of smoke farted from the van's rear as Chloe reassured her brother. 'See... the bluey colour in the smoke? It means it's burning oil,' she said. 'That's good. It's keeping the engine cool if it uses oil. As long as we remember to keep topping up with the thickest stuff we can find, we'll be in the south and surfing before dark...'

Chapter 3

The *Cote Sauvage*, it was called in French. The 'Wild Coast'. Chloe liked how similar the French for 'wild' was to the word 'savage'.

'Makes the ocean sound like it's gonna be really hard to tame, doesn't it?' she said, dropping the van into a parking space under the canopy of pine forest.

They'd made it to the coast just outside Royan, about an hour before sunset, just as Chloe had promised. Most of the day had involved passing miles and miles of flat farmlands. Fields had mostly been harvested, but here and there some late blooms had left stripes of colour across the land. Each small town could be seen long before you got there because of its water tower – an upside-down carafe of concrete.

The further south-west you go in France, the drier the land gets. It wasn't always that way, though. A few hundred years ago this region was mostly marsh. But then Napoleon had arranged to plant pine forests everywhere to soak up the water and make solid ground. At this time of year, falling pine needles and cones would cover the roof of your car while you surfed. Before they'd even unpacked their stuff, Chloe saw a pine needle slide under the windscreen wiper. *Better remember to take that out before we drive again,* she thought, *it'll scratch the windscreen if we don't.* 'Is my passport still in your pocket?' she asked Caio.

'Uh, yeah, it is.' Caio patted his hip. 'Probably the safest place anyway, isn't it? Unless you want it back?'

'Nah, you're alright. We just need to remember to lock them away when we get back.'

'I can do it now?'

'Nah – I'll forget the combination about ten times. Let's get moving. Waves and tide won't wait.'

The next part was a ritual: unfolding their wetsuits, unzipping their board bags, slinging their wetsuits over their boards and a towel over their shoulders. They were heading for the edge of the continent.

'Wind's dropping too,' Chloe said, nodding to the still trees up above. 'Surf's going to be good if that swell that went under the boat last night is still around.'

Caio wanted to see it before he got too amped.

'Remember to take a piece of Dad,' he said.

'Right you are,' Chloe said, and took a gentle fistful of dry ash between her fingers, wrapping it in a small piece of paper.

As they walked across the two dunes between the car park and the beach, Caio and Chloe could both feel the patches of warmer and colder sand between their toes. If the sand had stayed in the sun for the afternoon, it would be nicely baked and soothing on the pads of your feet. Sand that had been in the shade, though, was chilly. The contrast between the two was lovely, Caio thought. Not something he'd ever noticed at home. Chloe, meanwhile, had broken into a run up to the top of the last dune.

'Oh my god, am I *dreaming*!' she yelled.

In front of them was an almost empty beach and a lightly wind-groomed ocean serving up perfect waves. Darker lines in the deep blue-green surface were rising and spilling over as fast-peeling peaks.

'That looks so much fun, doesn't it?' said Chloe.

What a backdrop to the next part of the

ritual. They kept their eyes on the lines of raw swell as they waxed up and suited up. Caio, sensitive to the cold, was wearing a full-length, while Chloe was going for long arms and short legs, less cover – she loved the feel of water on her skin.

She tipped the little paper sachet of ash she had brought into her palm again, and Caio followed as they got their toes wet for the first time in French water.

Like before, they tried not to make too much of a ceremony. A faint grey plume blew downwards out of Chloe's half-clenched fist and mixed with the foam and sand as the first few bits of whitewater bashed their ankles.

'Sea feels warm, doesn't it?' Caio said.

They both made it out behind the breaking waves together and sat up on their boards. The sun, low in the sky and straight out to sea, made them shade their eyes with their hands to see waves coming.

'Here's yours,' said Chloe as a peak of water began to rise behind them. Caio didn't need any more invitation to ride the first wave of the trip. He dug his arms into the water and paddled towards it, swinging round just before the top of the peak pitched forward and the wave began to break.

He popped up to his feet and tucked his knees in as he took the drop, then transferred his weight to his toes at the bottom of the wave, driving his board back up the face. He cut a line midway up before turning back into the pocket. The wave drew patches of sand from the seabed and turned over itself quickly. Caio rode on towards the pitching end section and then set himself to launch gently out ahead of the wave, glancing against the closeout and landing in the foamy water in front. The joy was on him.

Behind, Chloe was stroking her way into another one from the same spot on the sandbank. She rode the opposite way around to Caio – 'goofy footed', surfers called it – so she had her back to the open wave face. This was no disadvantage to Chloe at all. She lifted the nose of her board to make a little moment of freefall as she dropped in, kinking her back foot as she went. With her front foot already on the outside of the heel, her body twisted neatly to attack the wave, which was about to try and run-off ahead of her. Where Caio had raced across, though, Chloe found her speed from going straight back up and then smashing her board off the top sharply. A hedgerow of spray fanned out into the late evening sunshine above and she drew her body in tightly over the board as it dropped back into the power spot. With speed to burn, she repeated the routine three more times before ending with the same gliding floater as Caio had done.

For Dad.

And now it was time to get another ten each, twenty even. Maybe more. They weren't sure how much daylight was left.

A summer of working hard, not seeing so many great waves, a drive across the mainland and their mission for Dad made them put all their efforts into catching these waves as the sun began to go through the phases of yellows, oranges, pinks and reds that would bring the day to an end and the winter one more revolution closer.

Walking back, the sand was all cold now, and the shared bliss meant they didn't need to talk at all.

For Dad.

The cold only made the glow inside Chloe feel stronger and preserved the grin on her face. Caio was drawing pine-scented breaths – it had been hard work keeping pace with his sister, as usual. *The best of the best*, he thought. But did she know it anymore?

They turned their backs on the darkening

ocean and made for the forest again, still in their wetsuits, with their clothes wrapped in towels.

'That car park will do for the night, won't it?' said Chloe.

But where *was* the van?

Broken locks, just use yours! Caio could feel his buzz turning sour immediately. The nerves in his fingers jangled. Each heartbeat could be felt in his chest, sending a burning sensation to his head.

The van couldn't have been...

Could it?

'Maybe it's the wrong car park?' Chloe suggested.

It's not, Caio thought.

Chloe was looking around, and Caio could see her lifting her chin, widening her eyes. She had her shoulders square and was repeating 'okay' to keep calm.

'Look – this is definitely where we were,' said Caio. 'I remember leaning my board on that log while I got my wetsuit ready.' He walked towards the car park exit then broke into a jog as he reached the road. It was long, straight and flat, running up and down the coast, north to south for miles. There was nothing in sight.

They'd both heard of this sort of thing

happening before – in Dad's stories to them as children, for one thing. But surely not nowadays? And not to them? And not *now*, on *this* trip... with the rest of *Dad in there still*.

Chloe felt water in her eyes. She prided herself on being the girl for whom nothing had mattered. Who cared what went wrong? She had herself, she had the ocean, she had her crew of friends and she had family. Sort of.

But this was different. This mattered.

* * *

It was the slowest, most sombre change they'd done. Not when Chloe had competed and nearly won a European title, not when she'd come second on the last-but-one wave of the final, not even when she knew something she'd worked years for was probably never going to happen again had she felt so drained of happiness, so betrayed by going surfing. The salt water in her hair now represented guilt. Why had they been so stupid?

There was even a spare key under the passenger seat, thought Chloe. Could they have made it any easier?

Their dad's van, with all their stuff inside, including the last memento of the man himself.

And in a van with locks that didn't even work properly.

'Thank God I left those passports in my pocket,' said Caio. 'Doesn't feel like much consolation right now, mind.'

It was dark by the time they admitted what had happened and trudged onto that long, long main road.

'We should start heading south,' said Caio, as that was where they'd seen signs for a village earlier.

One set of headlights grew behind them then shrunk away again as a small car passed by. It was minutes until the next, and then nearly a quarter of an hour until the next. Eventually, Caio started putting his thumb out. It was going to take hours to walk to civilisation, so they might as well try...

The woman who pulled over – probably about the same age as Chloe – tall, very well dressed, with silky straight black hair – had good English and wanted to help.

'Oh no. This is terrible!' she said. 'I am so sorry for France that this has happened to you. You must stay the night. I will phone the police now and we make a report. You will have *assurance* right – is that the English word?'

'You mean insurance?'

'Yes. This. You get a report and then somebody pays you back for your van.'

Money? What use was that going to be? You wouldn't exactly be able to put up a cash reward for a flask of ash, would you? One Poundland urn, lost in an old VW camper.

Numb, they were eating a late, late supper of pasta, tuna, boiled egg and olives – the kindness mattered, of course – before going through the pointless details in a local police station the next morning.

'What does this van look like, please?' They watched the officer's eyes rolling as they described the lightning bolt spray, the yellow awning. Even if it looked pretty unique, nobody was going to search for this vehicle.

With their bank cards cancelled, they only had their phones with a day's battery. They'd be hitchhiking again. Another officer dropped them back at the edge of the A10, on the road to Pons, and there they were, among the shaved farm fields of Les Charentes, surfboards under arm, wetsuits in carrier bags.

Had they been in the country forty-eight hours yet? And did that dream surf session really even happen?

A crossroads: north to Saintes, Poitiers... Maybe they could use PayPal to wire someone money for a ferry ticket back? For Dad. But without Dad.

But then there was the opposite way. With nothing but the clothes on their backs and a board each under their arms. Also for Dad?

So they listened, sat by the dying-back hedges of another field, cars passing them from both directions. Listened for what? For his voice, maybe. To the memories in their own minds.

What would he do if he was here? What did he want them to do?

They listened, and thought. The answer was here, somewhere. It had to be.

Chapter 4

After their father Geoff's death, the ice-cream parlour had remained pretty much Chloe and Caio's only reason to stay in touch – well, that and surfing.

Growing up, though, it was Chloe being *so* good at it – and Geoff banging on about how good she was too – which had probably led to Caio playing it cool as a surfer himself.

Four years younger than his half-sister, Caio was always being reminded how much work there was left to catch Chloe. Boys should catch girls anyway, he was told. Well, in this one case, it never happened.

For most of their lives, these half-siblings had seen each other as having something the other wanted. Caio lived with his dad, under the same roof, but Chloe was the one Dad always wanted to go surfing with.

She was born from Geoff's first marriage, and Caio secretly believed his dad still wanted to be back with her mum instead. Caio thought it was why his own mother and Geoff also went their separate ways – when Caio was fifteen and doing his GCSEs. For some kids that would derail you completely. For Caio it was his motivation. He stopped surfing, stopped going out, got some of the best grades in his year and then set his sights on uni inland. It would beat working in the family ice-cream parlour anyway. How dead-end was that?

Chloe, meanwhile, was only *ever* going to work in the family business. She could get put in charge a bit, take whatever time off she wanted and still surf every single day she needed to. Living the dream. Apart from when she had to manage Caio, who still fell into a summer job there every year throughout his time in uni.

It wasn't her brother's work ethic that was a problem for Chloe. Not at all. Caio was super switched-on. Or maybe that *was* the issue, actually. Caio was the one guy she couldn't order around, unless it was in the water, where she was instantly top dog over pretty much everyone in their generation.

And then Caio got his degree and was in the trainee part of his new job – pharmacist. Hard work. Good shift patterns for surfing though, which he still *loved* to do. He'd be able to afford to travel more than Chloe. He was going to break that family tradition of working the tourist season and then surfing and lounging about in winter.

Then Geoff decided to break all the traditions himself. He got ill.

*　　*　　*

The challenge, as Geoff worded it, was this...

Caio and Chloe were spoken to in turn, each during a last proper heart-to-heart with their father in hospital. He was going home the next day, but everyone knew what that meant.

Home, and nowhere else.

Home, for a week or two, at best.

Chloe was first to be summoned. There was to be no mention of any of this once Geoff was back in the house, once the others were all around. She could talk to Caio about it only once Geoff was gone.

The challenge... Different for both brother and sister, but shared:

'That boy needs to live out some *risk*,' their father had told her. 'He's such a cool cat. I've seen that look in his eye when he's about to have *serious* fun. He knows he's got the taste for it. That's why he holds back. He's afraid of it. You're not, though. You can help set him free.'

The challenge. Different versions for each of them. Same goal:

'That girl has *so* much natural talent,' their father had told Caio. 'But she plays it safe. She's a homebird. She wants a party with her friends and to be the best in the water here the next day. You, though, you want to move in wider circles. You want to expand. You need to help her do the same thing.'

The challenge and the instructions were exactly the same:

'The camper van. D'you know how old it is? It's more than thirty years old. It was from Ten.'

Ten. This was a person's name. Ten was a figure who had always appeared in their dad's wild tales from the late seventies, when he and a bunch of hippies traipsed through Europe and North Africa endlessly in search of surf.

Ten was the man their dad had done time with in two different countries – for sleeping rough and partying on beaches. (At least that was how the bedtime stories went. They both knew it could have been something more serious.) Ten was the man who'd helped him meet and charm *both* their mothers. Ten was the man who'd rescued Geoff from a broken board incident, way out to sea during one of the biggest storms ever seen in Europe. Ten was the man who'd told Geoff to take a punt on the ramshackle seafront building, which had become the ice-cream parlour that supported them all ever since. And Ten was the man who'd disappeared without a trace one day, when Chloe was only a kid and too young to remember – when Caio was T-minus two months from entering the world.

But now, with Geoff seeing out his last days, Ten was back on the radar.

'I know where Ten is,' said Geoff. 'He's been in touch. He's heard about my situation, and I've had a message.'

Ten, the man who was now, Geoff believed, in Morocco.

'I want to leave him the camper van,' said Geoff. 'To give it back to him. And I want you two to take it to him. On a surf trip, together. With me there – in the only way I'll be able to...'

The scale of the task hadn't really sunk in at first for Caio.

But it did for Chloe. True to his word, Geoff never mentioned it once home, and true to their word, Caio and Chloe didn't exchange so much as a knowing glance. Not until the worst bit was done, until Dad had been celebrated. Not until it was time to discuss how to lay him to rest.

And now, at that crossroads in southern France, what was gnawing at Chloe wasn't the fact they'd lost both the van and Geoff. It was the other thing he'd said. The only other thing he did add to the mission information once home. It had come just two days before the end, before he went to sleep and stopped telling stories.

'Chloe. The business. Sell it. Sell it and go wandering. If I'd had more time, that's what I was going to do for us all.'

And the other bit he'd said. One of the very last things.

'I know you won't though. *Please* prove me wrong. I love being wrong. Please.'

This is why what they did next mattered.

And Chloe had made her mind up. But the hard bit was going to be Caio. Or so she thought.

'Caio. We need to carry on. We need to cross this road and hitch south instead…'

'YES.'

Before the last word had left Chloe's lips, Caio was on board. 'Of course we do. We've got to get to Ten anyway. We'll work the rest out from there. And also, if Ten's the legend he's meant to be, he'll probably appreciate the tale of how we get to him anyway.'

'What tale?'

Caio smiled, picking up his board and stepping out to cross the empty road. 'This one, right here, now. The one we're making with these steps.'

'Hang on then,' said Chloe. 'Let me take them with you.'

Adjusted to the southbound side, they sat again on their boardbags as the autumn sun just hinted at warming the land a little.

The next car appeared on the horizon. 'It's my turn to do the thumbing,' she said.

Chapter 5

'British plates. Leave it,' said Caio.

'Too late.'

'Aah, no.' Caio cursed under his breath as the black vehicle started to slow. He didn't want to be the type who pre-judges, but this car was ridiculous. Or truck, rather.

'These things should be Army-issue only,' he whispered to Chloe, as a pastel black, almost brand-new Jeep Wrangler Rubicon with tinted windows and alloy wheels drew to a halt at the edge of the road. 'Why does anyone need one of them to go on paved tarmac?'

'Ah come on, it looks like a fun ride.'

The engine stopped, and the electric window started to drop. A man in his thirties with round sunglasses covering half his face peered out.

'Surfers,' he said. Definitely not a question. Their boards were kind of obvious. 'And English.'

'Welsh,' said Chloe.

'Knew you weren't French, though. Even

though you've got no bags apart from that... wetsuit sack, right? Yeah, knew you weren't Frenchies.'

'How come?'

'Dunno. I just did. Where are you going anyway?'

Chloe started, 'Moroc—' before Caio cut her off.

'Biarritz,' he said.

'You're in luck,' said the driver. 'I'm driving all the way to Andalusia in Spain. Don't mind having some company for half a day.'

The man jumped out of the Wrangler and made for the boot. He opened it and started taking Chloe's board off her. Caio frowned.

'Thanks,' said Chloe.

'*De nada,*' said the man, smiling wide between his round shades and thick stubble. 'One of you wanna go in the front?'

Chloe made her way to the passenger side door.

'I'll do mine,' said Caio, picking up his board.

As he passed Chloe she whispered: 'Did you hear? He's going the whole way.'

Caio blew a silent *shush* at her. What if this guy turned out to be as much of a tool as his car suggested?

Inside, the air conditioning was chilly and

fresh, and the seats were soft and luxurious. Pop music from a local radio station floated through the air via top-of-the-range speakers.

Jason, as the man said he was called, started asking them all sorts of details, offering just where he was from – the south coast of England, near Brighton – in return.

In fairness, Caio and Chloe could see why their situation needed some explanation. The lost bags, the fact their only way of spending any money now was going to be if it could be done online. Even that was a short-term option, because of the absence of chargers for their phones.

'Sounds like a nightmare,' said Jason.

I wouldn't say "sounds like",' said Caio. 'It *is* a nightmare.'

'Look, guys,' said Jason. 'You have to let me help. I need to. Let me buy you guys some spare clothes at least. There's a mall off the road just behind Biarritz. Before you go and find somewhere to stay, let me do that.'

Chloe looked back at Jason, sinking into the leather seats behind her. She raised an eyebrow.

'And where are you staying?' asked Jason. 'Can I help there?'

*　　*　　*

'It's a guardian angel,' Chloe protested, hours later, as they lay back in a hotel room, pulling the tags off a fresh pair of jeans each.

'If it seems too good to be true, it often is,' said Caio.

They'd agreed to disagree on Jason – with one condition: Chloe's decision was the one which would stand. And Chloe's decision had been to tell him that they were going all the way to Morocco, and to let him help them. The plan had been discussed briefly while they stopped for a rest break at a services while still in the tall pine forests. Caio loved the way the French used the word 'air' for services: 'Aire de Labouheyre', 'Aire d'Onesse'. They made it sound much more of a change from driving.

While Jason had gone inside, Caio and Chloe had argued quickly. Like in work, or while surfing, Chloe made the call. Let him buy us some clothes but book our own Travelodge. Tell him where we're going, then stay in motels at the roadside wherever he does.

'As long as he doesn't go looking for a Hilton,' Caio had made her promise.

Jason's reaction to the news was delighted.

'This is a proper road trip now, but you guys are *mad* for going all the way down there without a plan. I'd have been heading straight back to Blighty. That's why I always pick up hitchhikers – there's always a good story behind what they're doing. Makes my life seem so ordinary and organised.'

'We do have a plan,' said Chloe, referring to finding Ten. 'And what's yours anyway?'

'Ah, nothing interesting,' said Jason. 'Work trip. It's boring. Your life sounds much better. Tell me about that European surf title you nearly won. I think I remember that. Were you pro for a long time? Did you ever meet Kelly Slater? Or Lady Gaga? That guitarist from Wham? He surfs in Britain, doesn't he? Or what about Chris Hemsworth?'

* * *

After a much better night's sleep than before, they were on the road again by half nine the next morning. New clothes, a decent shower – both Caio and Chloe felt like different people. Jason had stopped, true to his word, at the mall just outside Biarritz, before pushing on for another hour inside the Spanish border. They stopped for the night in a busy Basque town at the foot of the Pyrenees.

Caio still made them take their boards into the rooms, though, in case Jason drove off in the night.

'As if someone driving that thing would go to all this hassle to pinch a quiver of beaten boards,' said Chloe. Caio used the excuse that he wanted to do some repairs and clean the wax off.

After arriving in the dark, they stepped into the morning air and gasped. Top-lit by the early sun, soft sheets of mist were sliding up and down the steep mountain slopes. Meanwhile, in the foot of the valley, buildings and busy motorways jostled for room.

The day was warm, again, and traffic slow, even after rush hour had receded.

It was about an hour down the road when Jason's mobile phone rang in his pocket.

'Mind if I take it?' he asked.

They both waved their approval, and Jason lifted the phone to his ear. Caio had been expecting him to stick whoever it was on speaker and keep both hands on the wheel, but they were going in a straight line for now, so it seemed safe enough. But why wasn't the phone connected to the car?

'Yo, Jase speaking. What's on?'

The other end had a lot to say. Jason's replies were quick and sharp:

'Yeah... Yeah... I've already said that... No...

No... Yeah, I've said that, too...'

Caio and Chloe just looked out the window at factories and warehouses. North Spain was much more built up. They were going to go off this highway and south soon – so Jason had explained – across the central mountain ranges to the west of Madrid.

On the phone call, Jason was getting tenser.

'I've taken care of it. Trust me... No... I can't say any more... Well, let them... Look, I know...'

They could hear faint flickers of anger from the caller, too. Jason was rubbing his hair with the other hand, taking moments free from the wheel.

And then he hung up.

'Sorry about that, guys.'

His phone began ringing again, immediately. This time he ignored it – and the second call, and the third. This went on for several minutes.

'Let's pull in and find a drink,' he said, turning the phone off finally. 'Before everything shuts for *siesta*.'

Chapter 6

The mountains were mind-blowing. Thin, crisp air, cold and dry, with a sky so blue you could almost swim in it. Jason lowered the windows and turned off the air conditioning.

'Closer to being in space,' he said.

'What?'

'In space. You know, we're up in the sky here, in the mountains.'

Chloe didn't know Spain had ranges like this. She'd been to surf contests along the northern coast lots of times, but always straight to a hotel – often a pretty run-down, budget one – and then to the event on the beach. She wasn't actually sure if she even knew a word of Spanish.

Jason did, though. When they stopped for a second time, right in the mountain country, he got talking to a mechanic outside the petrol station who seemed to know him. He was completely fluent.

'He doesn't live here, though,' Caio reminded her. 'British plates on the car.'

Jason was accepting a cigarette off the mechanic and there was no rush to get back on the road. Caio asked Chloe the question they'd both been pondering:

'Where d'you think Dad is by now?'

Chloe sighed. 'Somewhere having fun, I'd like to think.'

'You mean you hope he's got a fun-minded car-jacker? Most likely thing by now is that they've handed the van on. With him in it. Most thieves like that would have a fence who moves cars into the market for them, re-sprays and does whatever's needed to clean the registration details.'

'You think there's a *market* for Dad's old VW?'

'I don't know, do I?' said Caio. 'People like them a lot, VWs. But usually they like newer ones, or they like the one they've already got.'

'Do you think they've fixed the locks by now then?' Chloe asked.

'Probably not. It's only been missing twenty-four hours, and that's probably a big job. You'd have to take the doors off.'

'And what d'you reckon they've thought when they found...'

'The ashes? Chloe, *anything* could have happened.'

Caio recalled that humble plastic flask Geoff

was in. If someone had picked that up by hand, then it would have definitely felt heavy enough not to be empty. And it wouldn't have sloshed like it had liquid in it either. Surely a clever criminal would have opened it for a peek. Flasks had no doubt been used to transport all sorts of substances along the surf trails of Europe back in the day, and in a van like that, too – so why wouldn't the thief open it to try their luck. But what would they have thought when they'd spotted what it actually was? Would they have realised? It was quite a serious crime to use human remains against the dead person's plans. That would have surely been enough to make most common thieves think twice, wouldn't it? But then, would that law have even been known to them?

'So, that amazing lightning bolt spray job, then,' said Chloe, staring up at the sky. 'It's going to be taken off? Done over?'

'Most probably.'

Jason was calling over to them and shaking hands with the mechanic. It was time to get moving again.

* * *

There were more calls to Jason's mobile as they drove. He'd turned it back on to send some messages at the last stop. Again, the phone wasn't connected to the car, so he took them handheld and Caio and Chloe could only hear one half of the conversation.

Again, Jason wasn't seeing eye-to-eye with the caller, who Caio and Chloe had now presumed was the same person as before. Each time, Jason answered abruptly: 'Yes?' 'Hu-lo.' 'What is it?' 'Yeah?'

Eventually, after listening to and agreeing several times with whoever it was, he hung up and turned his phone off again.

They all sat in silence for the next few miles. The obvious conversation starter – 'Who's that, then?' – was also obviously the worst thing anyone could say.

Eventually, it was Jason who said, 'Why don't we have some music?'

He started tapping the Jeep's dashboard display and found the option to 'Connect to a new Bluetooth device'.

Caio noticed their speed tail off as Jason concentrated.

'Right, what are you guys called on Bluetooth?' Jason asked. 'Have either of you got it on?'

'I'm "WASTEYOURTIMEONME",' said Chloe, 'and it should be on automatically.'

Caio watched Jason find the name and begin asking the Wrangler's navigation system for a code to connect with Chloe's phone.

'Why don't you just sync yours?' Caio asked.

Jason seemed not to hear him, so he asked again.

'Why not yours? Why don't you just connect that? It's your car, right?'

This time, Jason heard him and fired an instant reply, saying, 'Mine's broken. Bluetooth doesn't work. The phone got too hot when I left it by a window once. Hasn't had WiFi or Bluetooth since.'

The screen flashed up WASTEYOURTIME-ONME and a four-digit PIN code.

'There you go,' said Jason. 'Easy, Chloe. Just enter those numbers and that's the car's code. You can DJ the last bit of the trip for us…'

They were back up to standard speed now – sitting just 5 or 10kmh over the limit. Easing out into the second lane while Chloe looked for something to play, they flew past a lorry full of logs and the ocean came into sight on the distant horizon.

Chapter 7

Of all the corners of the world's oceans Chloe had seen, the luminous blue of the Gulf of Cadiz struck her immediately. A sea the colour of jewellery, and a warm wind grooming the gentle swell lines that marched towards the breakwater walls of the Port of Algeciras.

They had made a huge leap south in the last two days, and now it *could* be felt. The sun was stronger, heating the sides of their faces as they sat on a bench at another roadside café on the outskirts of the town. Rising and dipping, almost to the rhythm of the waves and tide, was a rich rustling noise – that of the breeze pushing through the tall, fat palms and the lower hanging bushes and trees. It was an air current that had begun in the Mediterranean, and it felt refreshing and fertile.

'I'm coming on the boat,' said Jason. 'I'll book the Jeep in. No need to go through the hassle of embarking as foot passengers.'

'What?'

'I'm going the same way,' he said. 'Got business in Rabat, so give me a few hours to make a meeting here and we can drive on, together.'

'Rabat! That's almost half-way across the Moroccan coast towards where Ten is,' Chloe whispered to Caio.

'I know, but...'

'But what?'

'Shouldn't we maybe be mixing it up a bit?'

'What d'you mean?' Chloe, standing, leaned in tight, almost talking over Caio. He tilted his sunglasses so they hung above his ears and stayed seated.

'If we're meant to be having some sort of freestyle trip,' Caio, 'should we really be doing nearly the entire journey in *one* car, with *one* guy?'

'Why not? Have you got any idea how easy it will be to hitch through Morocco?'

'Not really,' said Caio. 'Have you?'

'No,' Chloe laughed. 'But just because we scored a ride across the whole continent at the first time of asking, it doesn't mean we're going to get it so lucky again, does it?'

'Still,' said Caio, 'what sort of story are we pitching to Ten if we say, "So this one English guy in a snazzy Jeep Wrangler showed up, right by the road, and took us pretty much the whole way here? And besides, do we have to get there straight away, anyway? There's swell. You saw on the way in. And I could tell you were checking the conditions on your phone too. Why not do some surfing in Tarifa first? Those beach breaks on the west side of that town are meant to be amazing.'

Jason was back from inside the café and was asking them where they wanted to meet back up if he went into town for a few hours.

'Can you drop us out at a surf spot on the west side?' Chloe asked, before Caio could get there first. 'It's a *huge* favour, I know. But I want to get in the water somehow in this country before we leave it, try and have a little surf, then we'd love to come on the boat with you.'

Jason grinned and pulled the key from his pocket. With an electronic chirp, he flicked the remote locking open.

'What distance are we talking?'

'Tarifa,' she said. 'My route planner reckons it's about twenty minutes away.'

'Sounds good to me,' he said. 'There's a boat that sails from there, too, anyway.'

*   *   *

The waves were smaller than Caio and Chloe had expected, and the water also had a surprise chill. Warmer than Wales, but with much more of a bite than the spot they'd surfed in France. Peeling fast across a series of shallow sandbanks, this was pushing Caio's skill set to the edge.

Chloe, meanwhile, seemed to have a sixth sense for where to sit to pick off the waves which did run slightly slower. Or was it the agility and athleticism of her take-off? She seemed to have such spring in her feet the moment she was up and would skip across the faces, smacking tufts of spray out of the back of the waves three or even four times per ride, when most other surfers in the water could just about manage once.

Pretty quickly, they'd drawn the attention of a few locals. Caio caught a stare from one guy, before Chloe paddled past smiling, and the man's grimace eased.

'Your wife is the best surfer,' the man said, half friendly, half scornful.

'She's my sister,' Caio replied.

'It is the same thing,' said the man. 'Your sister is the best surfer.'

'Thanks,' said Caio. *'Gracias.'*

'De nada.'

They surfed for just over an hour, and all the while each of them was staring nervously back to shore, where their bags were sitting, covered by a towel on the middle of the dry sand. Paranoia from the loss of the van meant they were now ultra-vigilant for the tiny number of possessions they still had with them. Each time someone walked anywhere near, Caio would start preparing himself for a mad paddle to shore. He imagined himself running across the beach yelling 'Thief!' to nobody who knew what the word meant while they were robbed of literally the clothes off their backs. He wondered if you could get to Western Morocco in only a wetsuit. The blisters and dehydration would finish you off, surely.

Chloe was rolling her hair in her towel and wringing water from it as Jason's Jeep came back into view.

'We're all booked on,' he said. 'Went down to the ferry terminal in person, couldn't fix it up online. The boat is sitting in dock. There were a few cars starting to queue already. We're heading over in nice time though.'

'Your meeting go okay?' Caio asked.

'As always,' said Jason.

Boards and bags back in the Jeep, he turned the ignition. 'Who's ready to sail to Africa?'

Chapter 8

The boat was smaller than most of the ones that went between England and France. Its red hull, which didn't quite hide the rust, had a mossy tide mark a few metres above sea level. Was that how much the ship was going to settle into the water once it was full?

A lot of trucks were going on – mostly empty after dropping goods this side, on the European mainland. The standard leisure motorists were in the queue too, a group of German bikers, a pair of vintage MGs.

Caio was watching Jason closely. Jason was taking a lot of interest in his wing mirrors, Caio thought, and was twisting his cap around his head restlessly.

'You ok?' Caio asked.

'Uh, yeah, uh, I think I am. I get seasick. Even at the thought. I might need one of you to drive us on. I'll be back in a minute. Are we out of drinking water?'

'There's a big bottle here,' said Chloe.

'No worries.' Jason leaned forward in his seat and looked out the front window at the boat. 'Thanks. I need a minute anyway.' He got out of the Jeep and stepped away. 'Jump in the front, one of you? If they need to move the car while I'm gone, just drive it for me.'

He walked towards a toilet block to the far end of the ferry queue.

'I'm not sure about this, Chloe,' Caio said. 'Is it me? Something doesn't feel right.'

Chloe rolled her eyes. Caio had never left Europe. She'd forgotten that.

'Everything's fine,' she said. 'And he'll be okay, too.' She pointed to the direction Jason had gone.

*   *   *

It was about fifteen minutes before Jason came back, hacking away with a wicked cough, and wet from splashing his face.

'You feeling better?' Caio asked him.

'Not yet, really. Can you drive – just to get on the boat? It's the smell of the fumes once we get in, too. I won't sue you if you dent anything. Don't stress about that.'

That wasn't what Caio was worrying about. He thought it wasn't going to be a good idea to drive up to the check-in booths, here, without the named driver behind the wheel. Not when the people at those booths got to decide if you could leave the country or not. But Jason was adamant.

'I'm not feeling too great, guys. If one of you can't drive this thing onto the ramp, then I dunno if we can go on this boat tonight.'

Despite Caio hissing at her, Chloe held out her hand and took the key. The colour returned slowly to Jason's face as he curled up in the passenger seat.

'You better be sure you're not suing me if I jam this thing into a wall,' Chloe reminded him.

'I promise. Thanks so much for this. Don't know what's wrong with me.'

They were through the booth and into the next queue. The lowered drawbridge of the ferry was about thirty cars in front, and men in fluorescent tabards were beginning to beckon cars onto the boat. The row they were waiting in was going to be last on, and all the engines around them were still off.

Jason wanted fresh air again and was outside.

'Let's get out too,' said Caio.

Chloe flicked the key out of the ignition and opened the driver-side door.

'No. Stay there,' said Jason. 'They won't let the driver leave the car.'

Well get back in it yourself, Caio wanted to say.

It looked like Chloe hadn't heard Jason anyway, because she stepped out and stretched her arms.

That was when Caio noticed three officers walking towards them. They weren't in police outfits, so he presumed customs. *Great,* he thought. *What a nightmare.* They had nothing to hide, though, but still...

Jason stepped back and looked around as the middle officer arrived in front of them.

'Who is the driver of this car?' the officer asked.

'She is,' said Jason.

The officer turned to Chloe. 'Can you confirm the registration please? Is this one correct?' He pointed to the UK plates on the car.

'Er, I'm just at the wheel,' said Chloe. 'It's his car.'

Jason made a sharp intake of breath. 'No, it's not!' he yelled. 'What are you trying to say?'

Chloe looked blankly at him. Caio's blood froze.

One of the other two officers spoke into his radio, his tone urgent.

'The registration you have there does not match this car's model,' said the first officer. 'It is not for a Jeep. Whose is this car?'

'His.' Chloe pointed at Jason.

'No, it's not,' said Jason again. 'These guys picked me up hitchhiking. *It's theirs.*'

A group of uniformed men were now coming out of the building behind them and approaching briskly.

'We will need you all to come with us.'

'What d'you mean?' asked Caio.

'She's got the key in her hand there,' said Jason. 'Look.'

Chloe looked down absent-mindedly at the same time as the officers did. There, sure enough, as she knew it would be, was the key to the Wrangler in question.

Jason continued, red faced. 'Have they done something wrong? I'm nothing to do with them. She's got the keys, and if you don't believe me, look whose phone is connected to it. It's her's. This is *their* car.' He wagged his hand at both Caio and Chloe.

They were completely encircled by the uniformed men now.

Caio looked at Jason and tried to make eye contact. Had he gone mad?

Jason continued pleading to the customs

officers: 'I've changed my mind now,' he said, his voice trembling. 'I don't want to go on this boat with them anymore. I'm going back to the town. They picked me up this morning, and I haven't got anything else to do with them.'

Caio felt anger wash over him: 'You lying piece of...'

'Wow!' Jason yelled. 'Don't let him hurt me.'

'All of you wait there,' said the lead officer. 'You will all be arrested in a minute, but if you try to leave now, it will be worse.'

Chloe turned to look at Caio, then at the officers. She felt a knot in her stomach, her heart thumping, as it tried to flush the growing fear through her body.

Chapter 9

The officers were gentle with them, but it felt like things could turn in a flash. Jason had been taken away to another room and Caio was insisting that Chloe didn't go anywhere alone.

'If you've got access to UK records – or even just French ones – you can look us up yourself,' he said. 'We crossed the English Channel three days ago. I can give you the boat, our names, and the car we were in. It got *stolen* though. So *we* had a lift from *him*.'

'If you're telling a lie, we will find out,' said the officer.

'Run the checks then!' Caio declared. 'Plus, we can phone someone, right? And until there's a few women police or customs here, my sister is *not* going out of my sight.'

'So you were going to try to go to Morocco without passports?' the lead officer asked. 'You would have been stopped before going on the boat anyway. And you have good luck if we stop you here. In Morocco this would have been jail.'

'No. Our passports were the only things that weren't taken apart from our surfboards and wetsuits.'

'This sounds like a very good piece of luck,' said the officer.

'*Really* lucky, yeah.'

'Too lucky?'

Caio wanted to swear, to swing a blow even. He caught the emotion quickly, though, and forced it back down.

'Is someone going to tell us why this is happening, anyway?' he asked. He looked at Chloe. She was giving away nothing. If she was worried, then she had a knack for managing to hide it. She shrugged her shoulders at him.

'One of you,' said the officer, 'has driven a car which has been stolen in London four days ago. We know where it was going.'

'Well, it's the other guy you've got in there,' said Caio. 'Jason! You need to be speaking to *him*. We can prove we were both in France, driving a VW Kombi, when that happened. How can we possibly be jacking Jeeps in London when we're near Royan having our own car stolen?'

'How can you prove who you are?' asked the officer. 'You have only your phones? One of them is recognised by the car too, from when you were driving it.'

'That doesn't mean *anything*.' Chloe spoke up. 'Jason made me connect my phone for some music, because he said his didn't work.'

Now they could both see the potential trick that Jason had been playing.

'I already told you,' said Caio. 'We've got our passports. You just need to let us go into the car to get them.'

'*We* will find them if they are there,' said the officer. 'The search will be done by the morning.'

'So where are we going now, then?' Caio asked.

He and Chloe both knew the answer, though.

* * *

Caio didn't *want* to be disappointed with the cell he was given. If he was going to have a wild tale of Spanish jail to tell, it might as well be authentic, he thought. But nonetheless it was a disappointment.

The space he was given was more like a budget hotel room than a custody enclosure. Geoff and Ten's reports of Spanish and French cells from back in the day were hideous. Concrete without carpet, paint or plaster.

Buckets for toilets. Mosquitoes. Inmates who might kill you in the night. Caio thought about all the innocent people in the world who'd had to sit in those sorts of squalid conditions, just because luck or politics needed them to. It must take such strength not to go mad. Here, though, there was even a twenty-four-inch TV fixed to a wardrobe door, although Caio wasn't sure if it worked. Yet again, he was going to be a failure. *Yes, Dad, I'm locked up abroad. No, I still haven't broken down by the roadside yet. But I am locked up abroad. What's it like? Er... Well, it's like a hotel room really.* He could feel Geoff frowning at him from the next life.

There would be guards in a little foyer outside, and he couldn't leave – that was grim enough. But then Chloe was only next door, and his room was carpeted and furnished for reasonably comfortable living. He hoped that didn't mean it was designed for people to stay in for a long time.

The border control officers – for that was what the Spanish on their uniforms had meant, he now knew – had taken his phone away, so doing any research into the situation was going to be impossible, for now. He wondered how often this room got used – if maybe this port needed half-decent holding rooms for when they held asylum seekers, for processing, or other similar situations. On their way to the block they were in, it hadn't looked like there were any lights on.

After a quick chat with Chloe, still in front of the officers who'd arrested them, they'd decided not to use a lawyer of any kind until they were going to be properly interviewed. For now, they both thought the best tack would be to act really helpful – to plead for help, rather than plead their innocence. They imagined Jason, detained somewhere else, ranting and raving horrible lies about how they were the car thieves and he was just an innocent hitchhiker.

It was clear now. He had picked them up with a clear purpose in mind: human shields if he got into trouble with the police. Caio and Chloe were intended to be framed as the people in possession of the car. The phone trick with the music system was just part of it.

It couldn't all work, though, could it?

In the morning, they were summoned for another meeting with the head officer. That meeting was back in the other, bigger port town on the Strait of Gibraltar – Algeciras, where they'd first arrived on the coast the day before. To get there, they were taken together in a police car. From the back seats, they watched the reverse of the journey they'd taken with Jason. Yesterday it had been the glorious last few miles before surf. Today it was captivity. They wound through some rolling hills before the ocean came back into view again.

Cruising through the traffic, the car took them to the centre of the port system, much bigger than the one in Tarifa. They saw a ferry bound for Africa, with its expectant queue of cars rolling on, before they pulled up to a three-story office building and were taken upstairs. The officer who'd led their arrest last night was waiting, his hair brushed neater, and in a tighter, fresher uniform.

This time he gave them his name and offered drinks: Perrier water or Orangina. Chloe decided that was a good sign.

'I am Joao Romano, and I am responsible for this border with North Africa,' he explained. 'We still have the other man from the car in another interview, and I have more simple questions for you today.'

'Did our passports show up in the car?' Chloe asked.

'No.'

Had they heard him right?

'No?'

'No. Your passports were not in the car.'

'What?' Caio's blood froze. He tried again:

'Our passports were *not* there? So they're lost?'

'They're not lost,' said Joao calmly. 'They were in the bin, at the bathrooms just before the check-in zone.'

Caio and Chloe's both jumped to tell Joao why, but he held up a hand, calmly, kindly.

'We know you didn't do *that*,' he said.

'So are they safe now?' Caio asked.

'Of course,' said Joao, toneless, matter of fact. 'I need to know the details of the vehicle you reported stolen in France, and when this happened. I want to search if it shows us that you could not be in London stealing the Jeep we have in our yard today.'

'Where d'you want to begin?' Caio leaned forward in his seat, took a sip of water and anticipated the chance to start talking.

'I want you to begin with the day you alighted in France, and the sailing. We will also share records with the ferry company to check this.'

'Great. Share all you like.'

Caio did most of the talking, with Chloe chipping in when he left something out – or if he drifted into giving information that wasn't needed. It wasn't long before the details were flowing. Caio was gaining momentum as he and Chloe started climbing the rope ladder out of the hole they were in.

They laid out the whole itinerary of their trip far: the date and time of their crossing to France, their trip south and then west towards the coast, the waves, the fact their Kombi was stolen. They told Joao *how* it was stolen – *just use your own key* – and which police station they'd reported it at.

And they told him about Geoff's ashes, in that anonymous Poundland flask, sitting at the mercy of whoever was probably stripping their father's beloved surf mobile as they spoke.

Joao listened, wrote occasionally, and then reached into his back pocket. Caio and Chloe's passports landed with a light tap on the table between them.

'You are not going anywhere yet,' said Joao. 'But you can see that these are safe, at least. We will keep them for you, but nothing will happen to them if you are telling the truth.'

'Thanks, I suppose?' said Caio. 'I don't see why we can't leave, though? Not once you know it was that other guy, Jason, who picked *us* up in the stolen Jeep.'

'Trust me,' said Joao, 'and if you are telling the truth, it will be fine. We are stopping our interview now.'

Chloe turned to Caio as soon as the office was gone. 'Trust him?' he said. 'The trouble is, do you?'

'I dunno,' said Chloe. She shifted to sit sideways, facing Caio. She crossed one leg over and put an elbow on the table. 'Thing is, you saw how crafty Jason was when it all hit the fan back there. How do you know he doesn't have these police in his pocket by the time he's finished talking to them?'

'You don't,' said Caio. 'But what other option do we have? And anyway, this is Spain. They have decent salaries and solid pensions. What would be in it for police to blow big cases by taking bribes, or aiding and abetting petty car thieves?'

'Is this *petty* theft, though?' said Chloe. 'What are those Jeeps worth? It was like pretty much brand new. I bet it would have been fifty grand, new, and easily half that to sell hot to the right person.'

'More hassle than an honest living if you ask me.' Caio stood up and stretched before sitting down again, this time more upright.

'Haven't you heard of those sorts of cars getting stolen to order?' said Chloe. 'Driven down this way then shipped off to the Middle

East and elsewhere – once someone can get the car to a country that doesn't check it properly on the way out.'

'They checked it properly here.'

'Yeah,' said Chloe. 'But that was a bit of luck, wasn't it? I mean, they almost didn't. We were almost on that boat. Worth the risk, don't you think? If it's easier to clean a stolen car up and ship it out of Morocco... Well... if *we* were almost there, it means *he* was almost there, too.' She shuddered to think what their fate could have been if they'd made it over the Strait of Gibraltar with Jason. He could have had anything planned.

'And also,' she added, 'looks like he had a backup plan for what would happen if they checked the car details at the ferry anyway – us!'

Joao was coming back into the room with another tall, shaven-headed younger man, who was dressed down. Although it was the same uniform, his shoulder badges were unbuttoned, as if was at the start or end of a shift. He had a plastic zip bag in his hands with several documents in it and a ring of car keys.

'This is Iban,' said Joao.

Iban pulled out the ring and started rotating each key. Then he settled on one key, slid it out of the ring and put it on the desk.

Caio and Chloe held back the rush of adrenaline. Joao looked at them and smiled.

'Do you know this key?'

Of course they knew it.

'That's the one from our Kombi, isn't it? The spare? The one that was under the seat?' Chloe hoped Joao wasn't going to judge them on their stupidity for leaving it there in the first place.

'I believe it will fit a vehicle we took yesterday, if you want to try,' said Joao.

*   *   *

Both men led them out to a small golf-cart-style buggy and told them to hop on. The four of them scooted across the dock area, east this time. Long roads ran between warehouses and the occasional quay. It took nearly twenty minutes, with the buggy pushing its top speed. Leaving the port area, they then turned towards a car impound with spiralling barbed wire along its fifteen-foot perimeter fence. Another uniformed man waved them up to the double gates of the entrance and they walked in with Joao. The black Jeep Wrangler they'd arrived here in was freshly parked up, with three plastic documents taped inside its windscreen, each of them filled in with a drywipe marker. It was both haunting and fascinating to see the car that had gotten them into this mess looking so sorry for itself, so lonely, and so inert.

And then they rounded the corner of a row of towering RVs at the back of the pound, and right in front of them, in the mid-morning sun, shone that familiarly horrid clash of yellow, blue and orange, with the racing-striped awning and lightning bolt spray. There was no mistaking it.

'What the...' Chloe's hands went to her temples in disbelief.

Caio drew a quick breath of joy, then went straight to practical matters: 'Is it okay?'

'Look for yourselves,' said Joao.

'Where did it... How did it...'

'I wasn't working when this was found. It was near here – the driver probably drove it to the queue for a boat and then left it and went on as a foot passenger. It was, how do you say, abandoned? Probably somebody going to Tangiers, too, like you. But they were going on one of the boats from here, instead of Tarifa. This abandonment of cars before crossing to Morocco happens a lot.'

'We are all very lucky today,' Iban said. 'Normally returning a stolen car from England or France to its owners is very hard. You have arrived in a stolen car, and now you will leave in one – but you will make it one for one, so this is okay.'

'Now you can finish this with Iban,' Joao said, gesturing towards his colleague. 'First you will need to do some papers to prove you are the owners of this van, but then you will be allowed to go in a few days.'

'What's happened to the man we came with?' asked Chloe.

'He will be staying with us for now,' Iban said, making a cuffed-hands shape and winking. 'There are a lot of men who try to move cars from Europe across here to sell them in the rest of the world. They used to put them in containers here, but now we have better customs officers.'

'Thank you,' said Joao, tapping Iban on the shoulder. Caio and Chloe chuckled kindly.

'So, because we are inspecting what is inside containers much more often now, they take the cars to Tangiers first and do the shipping from there. Your friend will have to stay and probably make a deal to tell us more about the organisation he is working for before he is maybe extradited or maybe faces the justice here.'

'He's not our friend,' said Caio.

'I know. I am calling him this to be funny. Sorry, I'm not very good at it.'

'You're fine,' said Chloe. 'Can we have a look in the van?'

'You must be quick,' said Iban. 'Papers must be done, but you can look quickly.'

Joao was leaving, and for a moment Chloe wanted to hug him, but then saw that it might not be his chosen way of saying goodbye. Instead, she made a salute, which made him and Iban both laugh.

And then brother and sister were sliding the unlocked door of Geoff's Kombi open, both of them only thinking one thing.

He was there.

In the pouch behind the front passenger upholstery, right where they'd left him. At a glance it was *all* just as they'd left it. There were even the pine-needles stuck under the windscreen from the forest where they'd lost it, and a few more inside the driver's door which must have fallen through while it was being taken.

'Was this also delivered to Tangiers for an order?' asked Caio.

'I do not think so,' said Iban, immediately. 'They left it. This was people like you, probably.

Travellers. It was a good way to get from France to Spain, and then they will probably take another one once they are in Africa. Some travellers are not as kind to each other. I cannot explain to you with any sureness why they took this where they did, or where they were going. I can only guess. But they are probably in Morocco now.' His face broke again into his clever, kind smile. 'And also, I do not think that somebody is going to *order* this from a criminal organisation. The Jeep you saw, yes, but *this*? Please do not be offended to hear me say it. I have probably seen bicycles which I would prefer to steal.'

'That's fine,' said Caio. 'You guys can say *anything* you like about this van, mate. Anything.'

Chapter 10

The thundering sound of the boat engines underfoot felt almost like the last moments of a curse lifting. Late morning, and the warming day was yet to pull a wind in from the cool ocean. A soft, low-lying mist was causing Tangiers to fizz gently on the horizon, behind a sea of brilliant reflected sunshine. For over a week that faint landmass had been tantalising them, some days so clear it looked like you could swim there, other days behind a blanket of cloud.

Nights in a new budget hotel had racked up. Not jail this time, but not paid for either. They needed to be back in the van to afford their trip. But paperwork was paperwork.

In one way, it gave them time to sort out basics like finding new chargers for their phones – still their only method of paying for things. In the week that followed, they'd gone to a bank, logged into their own accounts online and then had help withdrawing. It was also time to bite the bullet and get that side lock fixed. *Sorry, Geoff.* Caio hoped he wasn't too much of a disappointment as he booked the van in at a garage behind the port.

'And an oil change,' added Chloe. 'Remember that bluey grey smoke is our friend. Who knows how the interim owners treated it.'

Along with the lock, that took a few more days, until one afternoon a mechanic phoned them in broken English to confirm it could be collected in the morning. A new set of keys had been cut and set for the doors, but the original would still work for the ignition. That meant the key they'd had the whole time – because it was in Chloe's wetsuit when the van was first stolen and the one from under the door could still be reunited in gainful employment for the rest of the trip.

The boat turned from being side-on with the enormous wharf and harbour wall to facing Africa and accelerating. With another shove from the engines below, their grip on the edges of Europe began to slip away and they were at sea.

'Can you actually believe this is happening?' Chloe said, turning her face towards the bow and feeling the onrush of salty air in her face. 'I kind of feel the most nervous I have about this trip right now. Dunno why, though?'

'It's been survival up to here, hasn't it,' suggested Caio. 'Maybe it's only now that it's really starting – our journey.'

Chloe thought for a moment. Wasn't it the unplanned parts of a journey that felt best? Passing days and days in a part of the world she'd never imagined wanting to see. Algeciras, with its mixture of industrial might and old European charm. Once the gateway to new civilisations, now a trading post between continents. It wasn't just a part of the world she hadn't planned to see, it was a place she hadn't really wanted to see. All her previous travel had been to surf contests, so she'd have transited through this sort of town without engaging.

But now they were back on the proper trail, and she wasn't sure what she made of that situation.

As they gained speed and Tangiers began to bob bigger and bigger in their view, she tried to count the days it was since that surf at Tarifa. It was eleven. Without being injured, was that the longest she'd ever spent without a surf? And why wasn't she missing it? It was going to take more time to get down to the part of Morocco where Ten lived, too. That was going to be the next time they could comfortably go into the

Atlantic without any risk to the ashes. Unless they took turns, maybe? She wondered, then, if that was overthinking things, now the locks actually worked again. Chloe reckoned it was nearly five hundred miles more to drive once they docked, and for some reason she kind of hoped they didn't do it too quickly.

Next to her, Caio was lifting his chin into the sea air. She wondered if his eyes were closed behind the black wraparound sunglasses. He was completely still, apart from a short tuft of hair, which was sticking out from the side of his head and billowing in the breeze made by the boat. They were at full speed now, and Chloe imagined that this still, calm, content version of Caio had stepped away from a shadow of himself before leaving the mainland. In that shadow was the other version: the worrier, the overthinker. At sea, moving from one continent to the other, he looked completely taken up in the moment. He wasn't thinking about what he was doing – which Chloe thought was the best way to do most things.

'Ready then?' she said, taking the Poundland flask from a bag. Caio gently leant his head into a nod, the only sign he was conscious.

'Just got to make sure it doesn't blow back onto the boat,' Chloe said, leaning a hand of ash as far out from the deck as she could. She released and watched a small grey-white cloud fizz in the direction of the ocean surface. Caio smiled and tilted his head away again.

The land ahead to the south was now closer than the land behind them. They were arriving in North Africa.

* * *

It was completely surreal to Chloe, behind the wheel, to roll this precious van, which she knew so well from home, off the metal of the boat and onto Moroccan soil. Immediately, the pace was different. Another gigantic port zone awaited, newer and busier than Algeciras, and she tried to guess how many of the containers being lifted onto ships might actually have stolen sportscars or SUVs in them. One less, thanks to the work of Joao and Iban.

The city was packed, but driving was better than she expected. The roads were well built and neatly organised. Nevertheless, Geoff's old VW needed to be gently coached through the stop-start urban traffic. The taxis and delivery trucks would have to give it the space it needed.

A series of interchanges soon took them onto a flowing highway, out to the coast and southbound. The Atlantic looked sleepy, a small swell running knee-high waves along stetches of straight beach for miles at a time. The waves were closing out with precision, crackling the shoreline in rows of ruler-straight lines before exploding trapped air out of the backs of the whitewashes.

'Not a lot of swell,' said Chloe.

'We've got time,' her brother replied. 'Weeks and months of it, right? Waves will come. Let's just take it all in, flat or pumping.'

She looked over at him in the passenger seat, one bare foot up on the dashboard and his sunglasses tilted across his fringe.

That's the way to see it, she thought. Maybe that shadow really had stayed behind. 'Shall we have some music?' she said. 'Too bad there's no way of connecting our phones to this one, eh?'

Caio grinned, said nothing, and threw a shaka with his right hand. The sun was now nearly square above the straight road ahead and all the promise of the journey was lit in its brightest colours.

Chapter 11

As the day rolled on, the high blues and contrasting yellow browns of the dry landscape were replaced by an orange sky. A deep red sun hovered on the hazy horizon before sliding from view on its way to the Pacific. Caio and Chloe had reached the edge of Rabat after choosing to drive on while the waves were small. They drew into a roadside petrol station with a wide car park behind it. A dozen or so VW campers or RVs were nestled against a cliff cut out of a pink-lit hill. They had all they needed: water, some bread and cheese and a stove to warm a black coffee in the morning.

'Can you believe this is actually our first night in this thing?' Caio said.

They'd been away for what seemed like forever, but they'd lost the van on day two – after sleeping on the boat over the English Channel – and only just got it back. Chloe walked to the petrol station to see if they could sell her a carton of red wine or something else to mark the occasion. But all she got was a chocolate milkshake, which they ceremoniously shared in plastic champagne flutes.

'To Dad.'

Sleep was rough but satisfying, and the coldness of the following morning felt like life was as fresh and charged as it had ever been.

They found a municipal beach, again with no waves, and waded out until they were knee-deep with another handful of ash.

Getting closer, Chloe whispered.

Despite being in jeans a T-shirt, Caio turned and dived himself under. He hung his wet clothes over a wingmirror as they had coffee and ate the rest of the bread and cheese. The bread had gone tough, but the luxury of the North African sun on their faces, the tingle as it dried the seawater off their skin, made it as good a breakfast as they'd ever had.

'Still no swell for a few days,' said Caio. 'Let's go south via Marrakech instead.'

'Plan!' said Chloe, and then, 'Where's that?'

*   *   *

Chloe was in another place she'd never planned to see, but this time she was finally seeing it *through choice*. How had she lived to this age, going on so many trips, and never before thought of coming to somewhere like this?

Her first recognition of Marrakech was from a surf movie, set in Morocco, where a few of the pros had posed for some lifestyle shots in the narrow alleys around Jemaa el-Fna Square – although she wouldn't have been able to tell you it was called that. The section couldn't have been more than forty seconds long before wave-rising footage resumed, but she'd always thought it was boring and wanted to skip it.

Now, though, stood in the same places herself, she realised the exoticism of travel. The first excitement she had felt going on an aeroplane to a junior contest in Jersey (where she went from airport to hotel to shoreline and back, with just a silver trophy to show for it) was back. The thrill she felt, one time, when a magazine took her to Ireland to surf a winter XXL swell with a camera crew (again, essentially airport–hotel–reef–home again) was here, in the winding arteries of the souk, one of the busy marketplaces that were must-see for many visitors.

The noises, the foreign tongues, the smells and the thin, high-altitude air – it was all combining to a buzz she hadn't even realised she missed.

And this buzz? It could be rediscovered *every day*, as long as you just kept roaming. Chloe was getting born again in the bustle and hassle of this town.

'Yes, miss! Yes, sir! Come. Good prices.'

When the call-to-prayer crackled through a megaphone on building roofs, cutting through the din, she almost felt a palpitation. '*This* is what I want to do in life,' she told Caio immediately.

'What, pray?'

'No! Travel! I want to see the world, like we're doing now.'

'Nothing's stopping you,' he said, warmly. 'If I had your surfing ability, I'd have got every mag and surf clothing company in the business to send me to far-flung places. Instead, I'm gonna have to get a sound job in some pharmacy and do it as a part-time hobby.'

'Why?' said Chloe.

'Because if we did this forever, we'd just wind up broke and tired.'

'Why?'

'We just would.'

'Why not use Dad's business?' she asked aloud.

'What d'you mean?'

'Well – everyone wants ice cream. Why don't we just get an ice-cream van and drive wherever we feel?'

Caio imagined what would happen if the fabric, furniture and spice markets of these souks were suddenly having to compete for their tourist money against a grinning Chloe in an ice-cream van.

But, even if she hadn't quite thought that one through, maybe she did actually have a point.

'Let's get to Agadir and find Ten,' he said. 'Then see how long our current savings last us.'

'Yeah, but seriously,' said Chloe. 'We could unlock more money any time – just sell the ice-cream parlour. Surely you must know Dad kind of wants us to do that?'

'He might want *you* to do it,' said Caio, 'but I never knew what he wanted from me.'

'Just to be happy, probably,' Chloe said with a wink. 'And it looks to me like you are. Right now. Doing this.'

*　*　*

They walked out of the alley they were in and back onto the Jemaa el-Fnaa Square – world-famous hub of busy trading, long lunching and deserved tourist pickpocketing. European, American, Asian and Australasian travellers strolled in, out and through the groups of local men in traditional dress. The scents of food, exhausts and perfumes floated through the thin air. At either side of the square stood little turrets, each looking out over a middle ground of canvas-roofed and plastic-chaired pop-up restaurants. Around the edges of the square were various entrances back into labyrinths of smaller shops and traders. This was a place for looking around, and looking up.

'The view over this place must be amazing,' said Caio, thinking of the people wealthy enough to head up to these rooftops for refreshments.

Chloe strained her eyes to the terraces above. 'D'you think the person who drove our van through France and Spain is somewhere here?' she asked.

'As good a place as any for them to be,' said Caio. 'We need to buy something funny for Ten.'

'Good call. The most useless thing we can find. But we mustn't get ripped off.'

'Easier said than done.'

They went back into the souks and set about looking at T-shirts. Every football team you could think of (except Wales) was copied somewhere, as well as various high-street labels. Chloe wanted something with character. A stand sold tie-dyed shirts and various Bob Marley livery, right next to a tailor who looked ready to take measurements for a company in the heydays of Savile Row.

They came across another T-shirt stand and Chloe started reading the statements. They were a popular American action sports brand, but obviously fake because of the fact that not a single slogan made any sense.

'They've been Google Translated from another language without checking,' Caio said, chuckling. 'Which one are we gonna get Ten?'

It was a toss-up between the one which said *'Don't go the way you want'* and the one which said *'What encore shows! 'When? Now?'*

They went for both, in a long haggle which also ended up relieving them of an extra couple of Dirhams in return for two Moroccan football shirts – complete with Arabic writing on the shoulders – and a bag of pink rose powder. 'For your skin,' the seller told Chloe.

'My skin's fine,' she said back, before passing the bag to Caio and taking the football shirts out of his hand. The seller and his assistant laughed hoarsely and from the belly.

'Reckon we give the powder to Ten too?' said Chloe.

'No way. This thing's like a bag that says "gullible" to all the other sellers here. Keep an eye out for a bin, will you?'

Chapter 12

One and a half thousand feet above sea level, this was a much colder night's sleep in the van. Chloe had won the paper-scissors-rock game for the bed inside the raised awning on the first day and now it was hers to keep. The next day, as dawn broke out over the Atlas Mountains, she looked through the little portal in the side of the awning at the rising sun.

They'd stayed on the edge of Marrakech for three days, and now, with waves due to roll onto the West Coast either today or tomorrow, it was time to descend back to sea-level. There were decisions to be made.

'Do we head straight out towards Essaouira?' asked Caio. 'That's the most direct route to the ocean, but also the straightest and the most plain. Or do we cut down, more towards Agadir?

'Let's surf somewhere else first,' said Chloe. 'It'll look better if we rock up with waves under our belt. What if Ten turns out to be some idiot who just blanks us and sends us on our way? That's gonna be worse if we've made a beeline straight for him.'

'He won't,' said Caio.

'Still, let's find our own route out there.'

They settled on cutting down through the mountains into a big valley, which came out at a small town called Imsouane. A fishing village on their map, Caio had heard of a friend scoring waves at a dreamy point break there.

It was, therefore, with bubbling anticipation that Geoff's old VW was fired up and taken on one of the last legs of its journey. A few quickly moving police roadblocks on the way out of the wider Marrakech area made them spare a thought for Jason, who they imagined was peering out of a Spanish prison cell right now, maybe even right at the Strait of Gibraltar, and the Moroccan coastline he'd almost stopped them reaching.

From there a series of deep passes cradled the road between several groups of higher peaks. Then they began to drop sharply towards sea level and that uniform blue horizon of the Atlantic Ocean began to swing in and out of view. An ocean with something new to its character: swell lines. While they'd been in the mountains, the great cogs of the Atlantic had finally come to life again. A thumping swell was bearing down on Imsouane, catching a kink in the coastline and reeling off perfect surfing waves.

Imsouane was on a rocky promontory at the foot of the valley. Terracotta roofs and plain buildings surrounded a harbour wall and several fish preparation warehouses. At the north end of the town, as they descended towards their destination, Caio and Chloe could see the full brunt of a giant swell. Waves were crashing onto a west-facing beach, piling billions of gallons of water into a horseshoe bay. Further south, towards the pier, the land was repelling the waves before deflecting them across a vast sandbar just in the lee of the seawall. The waves were peeling off for as far as they could see, to the joy of fifty or so surfers, all of whom were immediately in awe of Chloe's fluid approach to the long, drawn-out rides on offer.

From the moment they walked down the mossy slipway and paddled out alongside the harbour wall, Chloe felt a connection to this spot. Pointbreaks were always surf spots she liked to play with, but this one – sand-bottomed the whole way and with sunlit blue walls of water that went on forever – was her Mecca. She hooked into a wave the moment she left the shelter of the pier and was S-turning her way through to a fast inside section. This was her backhand, right foot forward, and the scope for surfing with power and precision was immense. As the wave rolled on and on, pushing her further into the bending bay, it began to draw patches of suspended sand into the face. The spinning sections sloshed the dark sand around as if she were scouring the seabed for gold.

Chloe finally kicked out into shallow, warm water and looked back at where she'd come from. Rows of waves were reeling down the point behind her and Caio was now up and riding too – on his frontside, which was the opposite stance. From where Chloe was now, the coast carried on stretching away into Saharan Africa. She was tapped into this new continent, in tune, its rhythms in her soul. Chloe watched her brother whizz down the line, tracking up and down the wave, lost in play.

The tide dropped back and the waves got better. They surfed for hours, then sat, catching sun on the dry ground in front of where they'd parked, then surfed again as the sun sank through the deeper layers of the horizon. The waves went from fiery orange to dancing oils to faintly moonlit before darkness called Caio and Chloe in.

Now there was another reason to wait before going to find Ten. They had found the pot of gold at the end of the rainbow.

'*This* rainbow,' said Chloe. 'But there's a world of *other* rainbows out there, isn't there?'

Chapter 13

Ten lived at house at the end of the road. That was actually the address Geoff had got for him. As Caio pulled the VW up onto a verge at the side of the road, he studied the sheet of paper Chloe was holding:

> Terry 'Ten' Endsleigh,
> Yellow house at the end of the road,
> Tamraght,
> Taghazout,
> Morocco

The journey from Imsouane to here had been everything it needed to be. Slow, winding, majestic – the road had looped and twisted its way out of the valley, hugging the coastline south. Half the time they were peering down into ravines and bays and half the time they were slinking in and out of semi-desert mountain country. A tree, almost bare, stout and round, was being climbed by a family of goats.

'Photo op,' said Caio.

'Nah, one for the eyes.'

'Fair play. You're right. We can probably Google them doing that if we want to see it again.'

A lorry was rusting, abandoned in the dust, and beyond it a troop of hikers, poles in each hand, were walking north to where Caio and Chloe had come from. Through the open windows they could take in air laced with mountain purity and the texture of the vast ocean.

The real challenge, once they found the buzzing surf towns of Taghazout and then Tamraght just beyond that, was going to be finding *which road* they needed to drive to the 'end of'. There were several short, dead-end streets to the beach, before a point break much shorter than Imsouane and then a river mouth. To get over the river, the main highway had to go back over the high point of the valley again. Here there were multiple little lanes going yet further uphill and inland, some paved, some not.

Yellow house?

That address had been good enough for letters to Ten to arrive successfully, Geoff had reckoned. Every time he'd written to he'd got a reply within a week or two, so he figured it was going to be good enough for Chloe and Caio to use too.

Was Ten expecting them? If he was, then surely he wouldn't know which month, even, let alone a day or a week. Caio thought Geoff had written to Ten to say goodbye, but he wasn't sure – would they have to break the news out of the blue?

They had enough ash left for one final send-off. Imsouane had, of course, needed a little ceremony – right down in the bay where that inside section drained gold patches of sand into the wave. They'd gone at the end of their last surf there, again during a bronze-tinted sunset.

Now it was time to get to business finding this yellow house, but not before one last sprinkling. After trying to ask around and struggling with the local mixture of French and Berber, they decided to just go to the post office. They'd know, wouldn't they?

The post office, dark, basic and empty, didn't have any idea. One worker behind the counter was getting ready to shut up for lunch. The only thing for it, then, was to methodically work their way up each trail that forked off the main road and see where they led.

They started on the beach side. It didn't

take long to rule that out. If Ten was living somewhere on a shoreline, it wasn't in this town. Surf lodges, restaurants and even yoga retreats had all sprung up at the ends of the beach roads, with infinity pools, verandas and gardens. They weren't going to be the scene of an old Hippy Trail wanderer.

It took three hillside roads before they hit on what looked like a good fit. A dust lane shrunk to a track so bumpy they almost didn't want to drive up it. 'We have to go on, though,' said Chloe. 'Even if this is a one-way trip for the van, it has to keep going.'

At the top of the lane was a disused farmhouse and a big field stretched like a quilt over the top of the hill. They were a mile up from the main road now, at least, treated to panoramic views of the ocean. The field had tyre marks cutting across it to where a new glass-fronted yellow house, two storeys and freshly painted, sat in the corner beside a lone palm tree. A white pickup truck parked immediately outside it was littered with surf stickers. Its driver-side rear wheel, though, was on bricks, and the windows were open. Was this vehicle in use? Someone must have driven it up here. Then Chloe spotted the tape across the front door of the house. She froze. 'Is that...?'

'I think it is,' said Caio, stepping gradually closer to look. 'Crime scene tape!'

The tape had been carefully placed across the front door in criss-crosses and wound around a gatepost. Yellow and black, it read:

'BARRAGE DE POLICE NE PAS TRAVERSER'.

Caio was on guard immediately. 'Is this for real? It can't be. I'm not going in there.'

His mind raced. Now he really wondered who'd removed the wheel of that truck back there and why they'd put those bricks in place. Was the person still up here, whoever they were? Was it safe to leave the van for too long?

'What d'you think has happened?' asked Chloe.

'God knows,' said Caio. 'But I don't like it.'

'Me neither,' said Chloe. 'We should go.'

'Too right.'

Quietly, as if tiptoes would make a difference when someone might well have eyes on them, they made for the van, Caio to the driver's side and Chloe as passenger.

As they passed it again, both took another careful look at the seemingly abandoned white pickup truck. There wasn't any sign of a violent struggle. Did Chloe dare look back at the house one more time, just to check?

They were opening the van doors, about to

turn away and drive back to sea level, when Caio noticed a man with spiky white hair watching them.

'Chloe! Look. There is someone in.'

He came down a staircase and opened the door, arms folded, a warm smile spreading across his face, and began gesturing as if to say, Come in, I've been waiting...

Ten.

Caio went to speak first, but Ten stopped him.

'I'm sorry to see you two,' he said. 'I really am. This means it's true about Geoff?' He held his hands out and Caio took a side-on handshake, before Chloe did the same behind him.

'It's true,' said Caio.

'Then we're all sorry for our loss.' Ten held the handshakes firm. 'And we'd better arrange a celebration for his life.' He led the way towards the door, tearing the tape away.

Ten answered the question before they could ask it:

'The tape keeps me safe from unwanted visitors. Just a bit of a joke. It means only people with a sense of humour can get hold of me.'

The smile that had welcomed them now had a hint of mischief in it which they both thought they knew from somewhere.

'As you can imagine,' Ten continued, 'I knew plenty of funky fellas back in the day, people I'm not keen to run into again in a hurry. The tape puts off the wrong people from knocking on the door. The bricks under my truck too. It's easy to fix, though. I'll put the wheel back on when I need to go down to the coast, which could be pretty soon from what I hear about the swell charts. You know you're not going anywhere for a while now, right?'

'Yeah,' said Caio. 'We know.'

Chapter 14

Not going anywhere had an important exception: the ocean. Ten's promises of a new swell were immediate.

'You think you had it good up there in Imsouane?' he said. 'Wait till you see the pointbreaks up the road from *here* when they turn on.'

He wanted to know a lot about Geoff's last months and weeks – when was his last surf? Could he still laugh? When did he last drive the van?

Chloe and Caio were quick to share with Ten the history of getting the van down to Morocco, too. Ten said he could tell dozens of similar tales of stolen campers.

'In the seventies and early eighties, you could sometimes negotiate getting them back even,' he remembered. 'Like there literally was an honour among the thieves. But that other guy you met...'

'Jason.'

'Yeah, he sounds really sinister. We're all into some scam or other at some point, but that sounds like serious, cross-continental organised crime. Even Geoff would have been worried about you for a moment.'

Ten took them for a walk around the plot he'd built his house on, past a backyard of wood sculptures he'd been making.

'I told your dad to buy land down here with me,' he said. 'But he was fixed on that ice-cream business of his. So in the end I said, "Geoff, you need to do that. Just risk it. It's what you want." To speak fair, he was good at it. But then he was too busy for a few years – not long after you were born.' He gestured to Chloe. 'And we didn't keep in touch. I only built this place four years ago, though, so he never saw any of it. Before that, I was living in an old shipping container, still up here. I told Geoff, plenty of times, to bring any of you out here whenever he wanted.'

Ten explained how he had traded pieces of land in the UK and France. It had been his knowledge of that stuff that had helped Geoff get the seafront spot for his ice-cream business for the right price and on the right terms. Meanwhile, Ten kept doing land deals until he'd generated enough to build and settle here, alone. Never married, no kids, and no regrets.

'It does make me think, though,' Ten added, 'when I hear about the guys from the good old days passing before their time. It's happened too much now already.'

They went out to the van together, Ten stepping gently inside as if it were a temple. The humble flask of ash was there, in the pocket behind the front seat. Ten felt the weight of it in his hand, untwisted the top and peered inside.

'Is this...'

Caio nodded.

Ten tilted it carefully and looked closer. 'You know how stoked he's going to be if we take this to his favourite spot ever? Anka Point, up the road. Let's do our ceremony while it's flat again, we can get into the lineup easily. Then we'll celebrate with waves later in the week.'

*   *   *

Anka point had got its name, or so Ten believed, from the ruins of an anchor factory on the headland. Ten also claimed the now derelict site, with its weathered pillars and fallen arches, was under plans to be bought by Jimi Hendrix at the time the singer died.

'Hendrix fell in love with this spot and was gonna have it made into a palace,' he explained.

'Half factory, half palace. On a bright day, I can see his music in the architecture.'

Ten stepped from one block of dust and sunken concrete to another.

'See the way the sun runs through these lines,' he said, pointing to a row of pillars. 'It fixes all sadness. Here, lean on this wall.'

They stepped into a blocked-off room that must have once been an office. The walls had fallen out from half-way up and there was no roof. Without wind to cool it, the ground was hot.

'Mellow yellows,' said Ten.

Outside the ruins, the ocean, resting again, gently flicked curling fingers of tiny waves against the point. The slapping sound of water on stone kept the pace of everyone's afternoon, slow and soft.

Ten had loaded his three biggest boards into his pickup, all of them way over nine feet, and they paddled out from behind the point at a rocky outcrop known as 'La Source'. They drifted across, back to Anka Point, and then around the corner to where they could see another big bay. If you knew where to look, it would be possible to see Ten's house on the hills behind. About a hundred metres from shore, much further out than the waves would ever break, they stopped, floated and listened to their thoughts. Then Ten took the last of the ash and tipped it down into the ocean. Slowly, it sunk away from sight, until the reflective blue all around them resumed as though it had never been interrupted.

'Watch if he doesn't send us one hell of a swell now,' said Ten, when the silence was finally broken, washing out the flask.

They paddled back to La Source, where knee-high waves were tapering along the edge of the outcrop and Ten stroked into one, holding the now empty flask in his mouth by the handle. Supreme, a style master, he arched his back and sailed along the highest point of the lip-line before dropping his back knee and jabbing the board into a sharp direction change. He hopped to the nose, one foot over the other, and held himself, poised in the curl, before lifting the length of board neatly over the wave and wading ashore to put the flask on the sand. Back on the board, he rose to his knees and started to paddle out for another. A man in his mid-sixties – maybe more – with the grace and poise of an adolescent.

'We can have a little mini-celebration in this stuff, mind,' he grinned, 'before the proper stuff comes.'

*　*　*

Believe what you want – and there's always an explanation for anything – but forty-eight hours later the three of them were back at Ankas, and this time staring at an awesome display of ocean power. From high in the North Atlantic a massive weather system had sent a dose of early winter fury. Caio and Chloe watched a set of double overhead waves, detonating down the line, as a queue of nervous surfers took it in turns to jump off the rock ledge and try their luck.

Caio and Chloe had boards they knew they could rely on in these sorts of conditions, so they declined Ten's offer to borrow any of the specialist pin-tails he kept for chasing huge surf. At dawn that morning, from the hill where Ten lived, the swell could be seen drawing its corduroy lines to the horizon and beyond. They hadn't been sure if a man his age was going to take it on. But Ten was as excited as anyone in town.

'I'm no use to anyone the day I don't go in when it's like this,' he said.

Good to his word, Ten was fearless too, leading them to the jump-off spot and then showing them how to leap into the cauldron of whitewater left by the wave before. Angling sideways towards the deeps behind, he paddled quickly and surely, missing the next wave by a whisker and then pushing on to the relative safety of the lineup.

Chloe jumped next, adept at what to do in conditions like this, and was hot on Ten's heels. Caio would have felt consumed by pressure in the past, he realised, but the difference now was that he *wanted* those waves for himself, for his own reasons. The thought of being compared to Chloe, of failing to be good enough... That stuff had indeed been shed, back in that pound full of stolen cars and the ill-fated Jeep that had brought them south.

A gap came in the sets and a wave drained its way across the rocks. Caio leapt over it and dropped his shoulders, paddling with all he had for the horizon and rebirth.

The swell was getting bigger. Each time a wave came down the point it felt as if the entire sea was moving with it. Caio looked back to land, moving sideways as masses of water heaved beneath him.

And then came a set bigger than anything so far. The horizon rose, and the darkening line of wave began pitching, way outside of the main take-off zone. Chloe and Ten, both tighter to the point, were going to be sent under it. Caio watched them calmly bail from their boards, pushing the craft aside and diving deep – right as a bulldozer of whitewater approached. Further out, a thin, dark-haired man spun around and dropped into the first wave. As he passed by, Caio could see the guy's board screaming to engage with the water. He looked down the vertical wall of water as the man raced off below, then the whole lineup was drenched in the spray tearing off the pitching lip.

When it settled – and Ten and Chloe were nowhere to be seen, somewhere under that whitewater – Caio spotted the second wave, and realised it would be *him* who was in position to catch it.

If he wanted it.

Am I here for any other reason? Caio asked himself. As he dug in and began to paddle, other voices and questions started swirling in the background too. His father was in there, somewhere, joking about the importance of breaking down in a car. Then all the praise he'd had to hear from others for Chloe's surfing ability rose to the surface and washed Geoff's voice away again. Were Chloe and Ten up for air enough to be watching him from somewhere near the dashed rocks inside?

He hoped so, and that was his last push of motivation as he sunk his shoulders for the final few strokes. He felt the bomb lift him, start moving under him. This was the moment. Stroke forward now and the only way off this mountain of water was going to be *that way*: down. The momentum began to build and he felt his paddle power give way to the freefalling might of his own body, gripping only loosely to the freight train of water reeling off to the side. As the board dropped away from him, he popped his feet into position, filling the gap, and then gripping from toe to heel. Leading hand low, back arm half-raised and with a gentle push of the front foot, he began to fall downwards, into destiny.

* * *

Afterwards, Chloe said it was witnessing Caio that gave her the motivation to push back out herself. She was getting smashed towards the rocks, drained of energy and facing the prospect of having to paddle almost to the next village to escape in one piece. But when she saw Caio on that bomb? When she saw that, she was so overcome with joy that she found the energy to paddle back out, right from where she was. She wanted one too. She knew there wasn't going to be another wave like Caio's all day – all swell, all winter even – but still, she wanted to get tapped into this spot. She needed a ride of her own, to mark the occasion.

Whatever Chloe did that day though, it was Caio's wave that mattered. Of course Chloe would get back out there, of course she was pushing over a ledge of her own not long after, and of course she was the star of the show, what with the backhand lines she drew on those huge, rolling faces – none of this was ever going to be in doubt.

'You don't need any of the titles you did or didn't win,' Ten told her that afternoon, back on dry land. 'You just dominated one of *the* iconic spots in global surf exploration. There's going to be people who'll remember forever what they saw you do today. Keep moving. Go and do it again, in other places. Or just stay here forever, both of you.'

He turned to Caio. 'And *you*,' he said. '*You* caught the once-in-a-lifetime wave.'

'Does that mean the best is behind me, then?'

'Never,' said Ten. 'Like I was saying to her, it's the once-in-a-lifetime wave for *this spot*, but there's millions more.'

Caio was kicking back with a bottle of beer in his hand, gazing out from the top of the hill, at the spread of waves approaching the points. Ten stuck his finger in the direction of due south.

'You can just about draw a line from here, right the way to Antarctica without hitting land,' he said. 'You guys did Geoff proud today. And not just today. Every bit of the way here, too.'

He turned a dried-out tree stump from a pile of timber upright and sat on it. Tilting his beer bottle Caio and Chloe's way, he added, 'So I'd better break it to you, then?'

'Break what?'

Ten swallowed his mouthful of beer, grinning as they waited.

'That van,' he said, laughing. 'I've never seen it in my life before you arrived.'

Caio looked to Chloe, who turned to the van, as if she expected another one to be pulling up behind. Facing Ten again, she began, 'But...'

'Nope. Never seen it. Never had one like it. Never knew your dad with one like it either. And he knew that. You realise what he's done, though, don't you?'

The kindness in Ten's face, the mischief in his smile – they knew this could only be going somewhere good.

'He *did* write to me one more time,' Ten said. 'Told me to expect you both. Told me to keep an eye out for that... jalopy there. And he told me what he'd said to you about it. That it was mine, from back in the day, right?'

'Yeah. So?'

'Geoff's last big wind-up, my friends. You've been had.'

Caio was a million miles away, but a glow of recognition started to arrive on Chloe's face. She thought of all those hours she'd spent, scared of telling her half-brother what to do when he worked for her in the ice-cream parlour. She thought of the awkwardness he would show her when it came to anything to do with surfing. And she realised the missing part of Geoff's final mission to the pair of them. The third component of the plot:

One instruction for Caio...

One for her...

...and the cornerstone of the whole plan had been sent to the man in front of them.

'What other excuse was he going to find for getting you two together and onto a road trip like that?'

Ten grinned, lifting his sunglasses off his forehead as the sky went from orange to tinted rose.

'You mean…'

'He's got his last request, hasn't he! *He wanted you two to get up and out of your town. Together.*' Ten nodded towards Chloe and winked. 'Well, in your case anyway.' He looked to Caio. 'And in your case… Your dad wanted you to experience the thrill of the road. And look how it turned out. You've ridden the wave of a hundred people's lives today, and your sister is the queen of the point for as long as she wants. And *that's* only the beginning, if you want to take this lesson to heart.'

Before Caio could react, Chloe was on her feet.

'I *knew* we didn't need to keep him and that van together,' she said. 'And I also knew he was up to something. So… you and him losing contact… that's part of the wind-up too?'

'What do you think?' said Ten.

'I think,' said Caio, 'that I still haven't broken down in a car by the side of the road. I think we should keep it until that happens.'

'It'll happen,' said Ten. 'If that's what you want from life, then it's not too much to ask. Or you could sell it.'

'Sell it?'

'Yeah. To fund the next trip. Because there's going to be another one. Unless you want to stay here for good. Which, like I said, you absolutely can.'

'Would we get much?' asked Caio.

Ten took a moment before replying. 'Who knows, down here. Never paid for a car in Dirhams. Back in Britain, though? They love a VW over there, right? It's got to be worth at least a hundred quid where you've come from, hasn't it?'

Ten's cheeky wink was straight out of Geoff's playbook.

'Glad to hear it,' said Chloe. 'But I don't think that's as much as we might get for a beachside ice-cream parlour.'

Sitting back down, she turned to Caio. 'What d'you think, then?' she said.

Glossary

Closeout/closeout turn: A closeout is a wave which doesn't peel along but breaks or 'dumps' all in one go. A peeling wave is also described as 'closing out' the moment it finally stops peeling and breaks all at once. In that circumstance, a surfer who does a turn off the final closeout **section** of the wave has done a 'closeout turn'.

End section: Another word for the final closeout part of a wave which has been peeling. Some **point breaks** can be described as having an end section which doesn't **close out** though, as they eventually peel into deep water. In that case, end sections may also be called a **shoulder**.

Face (wave face): The unbroken part of a peeling wave that provides the fastest, smoothest place for a surfer to be.

Floater: A manoeuvre which involves riding the surfboard up on top of the breaking wave, gliding or **floating** along it, then jumping back down.

Goofy footed: A surfer who stands with their right foot forward. Although not linked to left-handed or footedness, this is a lot rarer than being a **natural foot** and standing with your left foot as the lead.

Lineup: The area of ocean behind where the waves are breaking in which surfers sit and wait for the chance to catch a wave.

Lip-line: The crest of a breaking wave.

Natural footed: A surfer who stands with their left foot forward – by far the most common stance. See also: **goofy footed**.

Pin-tail: A surfboard with a pointed tail, specifically for coping with high speeds on big waves.

Pitching: When the **lip-line** of a wave is throwing out and descending as a curtain of water.

Point break: A highly sought-after surf spot where waves always break in a very similar place and peel in the same direction. These spots are usually formed around land-features such as points, headlands or sharp bends in the coast.

Section: An individual breaking part of a wave.

Set/set wave: Within a **swell**, a group of bigger or more powerful waves is known as a set. A set wave is a bigger, better wave that stands out from most other waves breaking that day.

Shaka: A hand gesture, thought to originate in Hawaii, with the thumb and little finger extended out from a fist. Shakas are a widely used greeting within surf culture.

Shoulder: The unbroken, and therefore less steep, edge of a breaking wave. Sometimes a shoulder can also be an **end section**. The shoulder is a part of the wave which is generally much safer, as it is over deeper water, so experienced or braver surfers will usually want to avoid being here too much.

Swell: A spell of good or big waves caused by a storm. Swells usually last days, not hours, and comprise hundreds of **sets**.

XXL (swell): A surf industry-sponsored concept where prize money is offered each year for finding and riding the biggest waves in the world with video or photo evidence. There is an annual XXL awards ceremony, with **XXL**-nominated waves and surfers. An **XXL swell** is a giant, few-times-a-year **swell** which famous or aspiring professional surfers will try to meet at one of the world's well-known big-wave destinations like Hawaii, Tasmania, Tahiti, Ireland and Portugal.